**W9-AXP-717**

# FRANKLIN PARK PUBLIC LIBRARY
## FRANKLIN PARK, ILL.

Each borrower is held responsible for all library
material drawn on his card and for fines accruing on
the same. No material will be issued until such fine
has been paid.

All injuries to library material beyond reasonable
wear and all losses shall be made good to the
satisfaction of the Librarian.

Replacement costs will be
billed after 42 days overdue.

# Caillou

## Is Sick

Adaptation of the animated series: Roger Harvey
Illustrations taken from the animated series and adapted by Eric Sévigny

chouette  COOKIE JAR

Today, Caillou stayed in bed. Mommy felt his forehead. "Hmm, I think you have a fever," she said. Even though he didn't feel well, Caillou still wanted to go outside and play with his truck.

Mommy came back with a glass of water and a little pill. "What is it?" asked Caillou.
"It's something to bring your fever down," Mommy replied. "Put your head on your pillow and sleep now. It's important you get lots of rest," Mommy said.

The next day, Caillou woke up and saw that he was covered with tiny red spots.
"It looks like you have chicken pox," Mommy said.
"Chicken pox?" Caillou repeated.
"That's right," Mommy said. "I'll get a nice bath ready for you. Then you won't feel so itchy."

"Your bath is ready," Mommy said.
Caillou knew he shouldn't scratch,
but he couldn't help it.
"No scratching, Caillou!" said Mommy.

"If you take lots of baths, your spots will disappear faster," Mommy said.
Caillou felt better in the bathtub.
"Are you ready to get out?" Mommy asked.
Caillou nodded. He stood up and Mommy wrapped him in a nice big towel.

Back in bed, Caillou rubbed his face on
his dinosaur.
"Caillou, were you scratching?" Mommy asked.
"A little bit," Caillou replied.
Mommy had a sheet of stickers in her hand.
"What's that?" Caillou asked.
"It's a surprise!" Mommy told him.

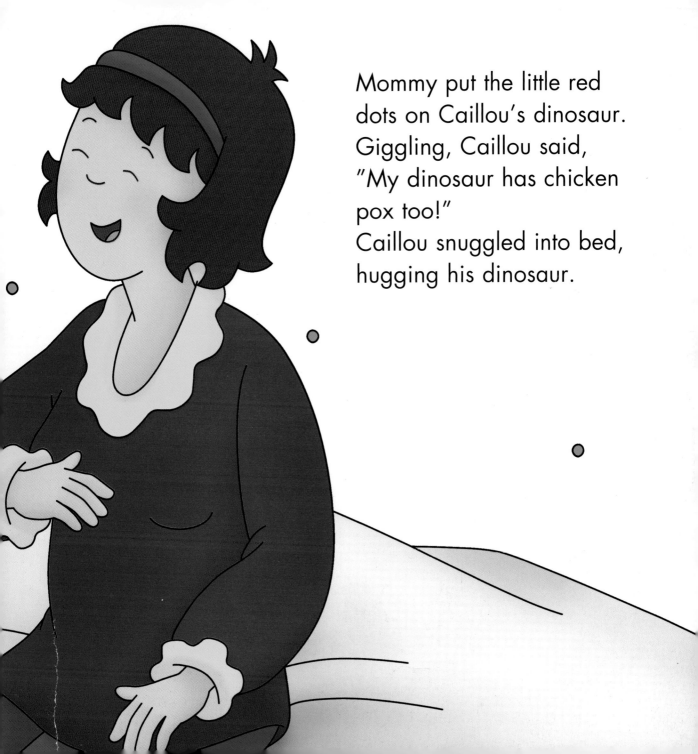

Mommy put the little red
dots on Caillou's dinosaur.
Giggling, Caillou said,
"My dinosaur has chicken
pox too!"
Caillou snuggled into bed,
hugging his dinosaur.

One morning, Caillou looked at himself in the mirror.
Yippee! His spots were fading.
"Mommy! Come see!" he called.
"Caillou, you're almost all better," Mommy said.
"Can I play with Rosie now?" Caillou asked.
"You'll have to wait until your fever is gone."

The next day, nearly all Caillou's spots had disappeared.
He picked up his dinosaur and ran to tell everyone the
good news.
"Daddy, look!"
"Oh, I see your dinosaur has lost his spots," said Daddy.
"Me too," Caillou announced.

"Rosie! Guess what?" Caillou called. Lying in bed, Rosie turned her head toward Caillou. Her face was covered with spots. "Mommy! Come quick!" Caillou knew just what had happened to Rosie. "Now Rosie has chicken pox."

Poor Rosie! Caillou felt sorry for his baby sister. While Mommy rocked Rosie in the rocking chair, Caillou brought her his dinosaur.

"Here!" he said. "If you take lots of baths, you'll lose all your spots, just like my dinosaur!"

Adaptation of text by Roger Harvey based on the scenario of the CAILLOU animated film series
produced by Cookie Jar Entertainment Inc. (© 1997 CINAR Productions (2004) Inc.,
a subsidiary of Cookie Jar Entertainment Inc.).
All rights reserved.
Original story written by Marie-France Landry.
Illustrations taken from the television series CAILLOU and adapted by Eric Sévigny.
Art Direction: Monique Dupras

The PBS KIDS logo is a registered mark of PBS and is used with permission.

We acknowledge the financial support of the Government of Canada through
the Canada Book Fund for our publishing activities.

Canadian   Patrimoine
Heritage   canadien

We acknowledge the support of the Ministry of Culture and Communications
of Quebec and SODEC for the publication and promotion of this book.

SODEC
Québec

Bibliothèque et Archives nationales du Québec and Library and Archives
Canada cataloguing in publication

Harvey, Roger, 1940-
Caillou is sick
New ed.
(Clubhouse)
Translation of: Caillou est malade.
Originally issued in series: Backpack Collection. c1999.
For children aged 3 and up.

ISBN 978-2-89450-865-7

1. Chickenpox - Juvenile literature.  2. Children - Diseases - Juvenile literature.
I. Sévigny, Éric. II. Title. III. Series: Clubhouse.

RC125.H3713 2012       j616.9'14C       2011-942122-4

Printed in China
10 9 8 7 6 5 4 3 2 1  CHO1819 JAN2012

9186010